THIS BOOK BELONGS TO:

____

Mountain Climber

A story about trying hard and accomplishing

By R. Kadosh

Illustrated by Chana Min Hahar

Mountain Climber

ISBN: 978-1-60763-369-3

THE JUDAICA PRESS, INC.
718-972-6200 | 800-972-6201
info@judaicapress.com
www.judaicapress.com

Manufactured in China

The gravel crunched under Rina's sneakers as she crossed the parking lot. She looked up at the trees ahead. They were tall and green and close together.

Rina's family was going on a special trip. They were going on a hike in the woods. Rina wasn't sure what a hike was, but her Abba and Ima were excited. "It must be fun," she thought.

Abba was wearing a special backpack with baby Chaim in it. Chaim looked surprised to be up so high. Ima was carrying a knapsack with their lunch.

As the family entered the forest, the ground changed to a dirt path. Trees surrounded the path, and the air felt cool and quiet. Rina could hear crickets chirping.

"Come, Rina," called Abba.
"We're going to hike on this trail
and go up to the top of a mountain!"
Rina hurried to catch up with him.

Uh oh! She tripped over a tree root.

Abba picked up a big, tall branch. "This is your very own walking stick," he told Rina. "It will help you climb the mountain and keep you from falling."

After walking for a while, Rina asked, "Are we at the top of the mountain yet?"

"No," Ima said with a smile. "You'll know when we're at the top."

Rina walked on and on. The stick kept her steady.

Suddenly she saw something bright move right beside her. “Look!” she whispered.

"It's a robin," Abba said. "If we walk quietly, we'll see lots of birds, and maybe even some deer."

Chaim giggled as another bird darted out of the trees.

"Are we at the top yet?" Rina asked.

"Not yet," Abba said. "You'll know when we're at the top."

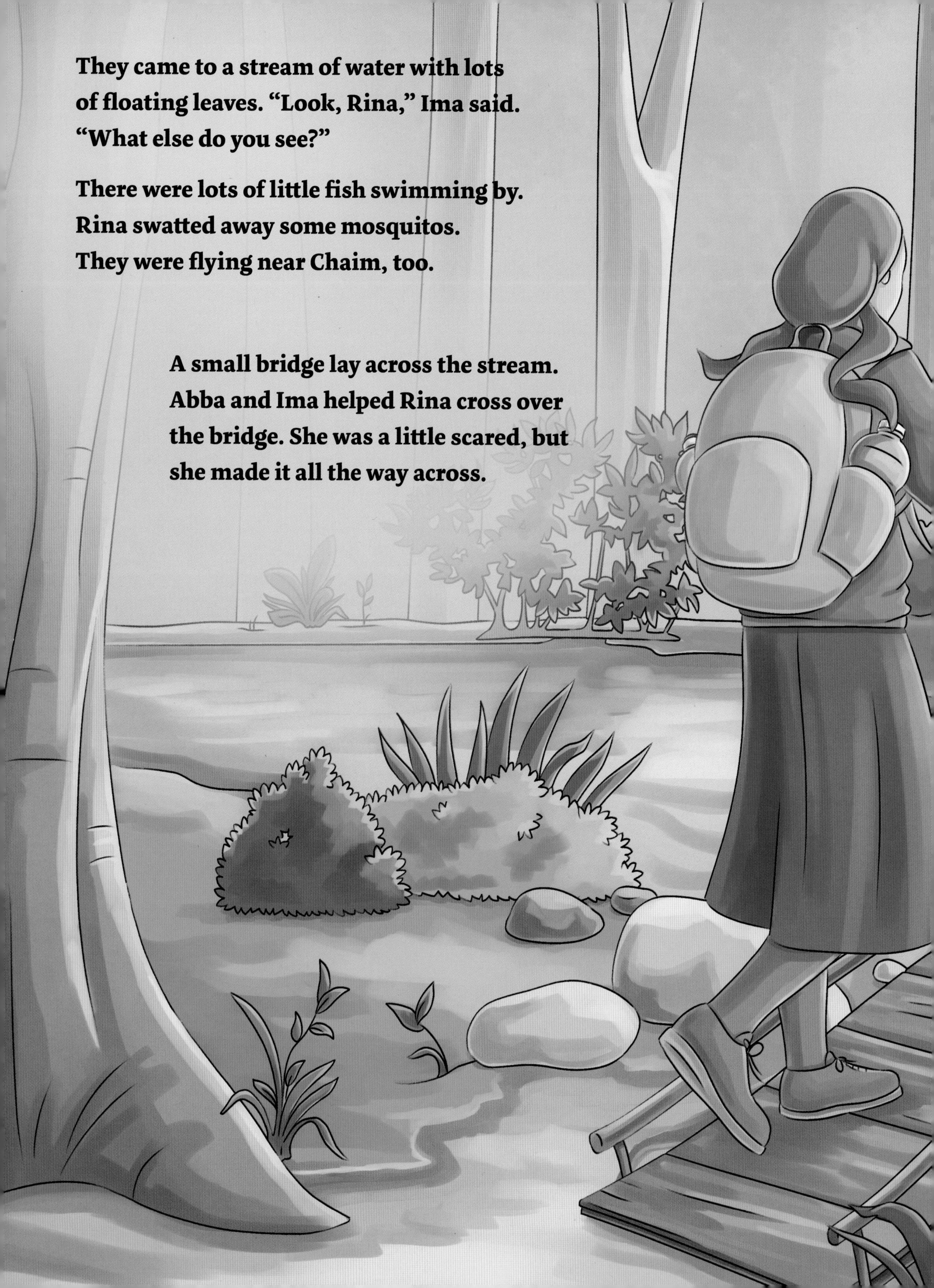

They came to a stream of water with lots of floating leaves. “Look, Rina,” Ima said. “What else do you see?”

There were lots of little fish swimming by. Rina swatted away some mosquitos. They were flying near Chaim, too.

A small bridge lay across the stream. Abba and Ima helped Rina cross over the bridge. She was a little scared, but she made it all the way across.

“Are we at the top yet?” Rina asked.

“No,” Ima answered. “You’ll know when we’re at the top.”

The trail got narrower and steeper. Lots of rocks were piled on each other. "Be careful," Abba told Rina. "We're going to climb up these rocks, one at a time."

Rina climbed. It was hard work. She was getting hot and sweaty. Ima held her hand, and she used her walking stick.

Slowly they went up and up and up.

“Are we at the top yet?” Rina asked.

“Not yet,” Abba said. “But each rock you climb brings you one step closer.”

“My feet hurt,”
Rina said in a small voice.
“I’m hungry and thirsty.
Can we go home now?”

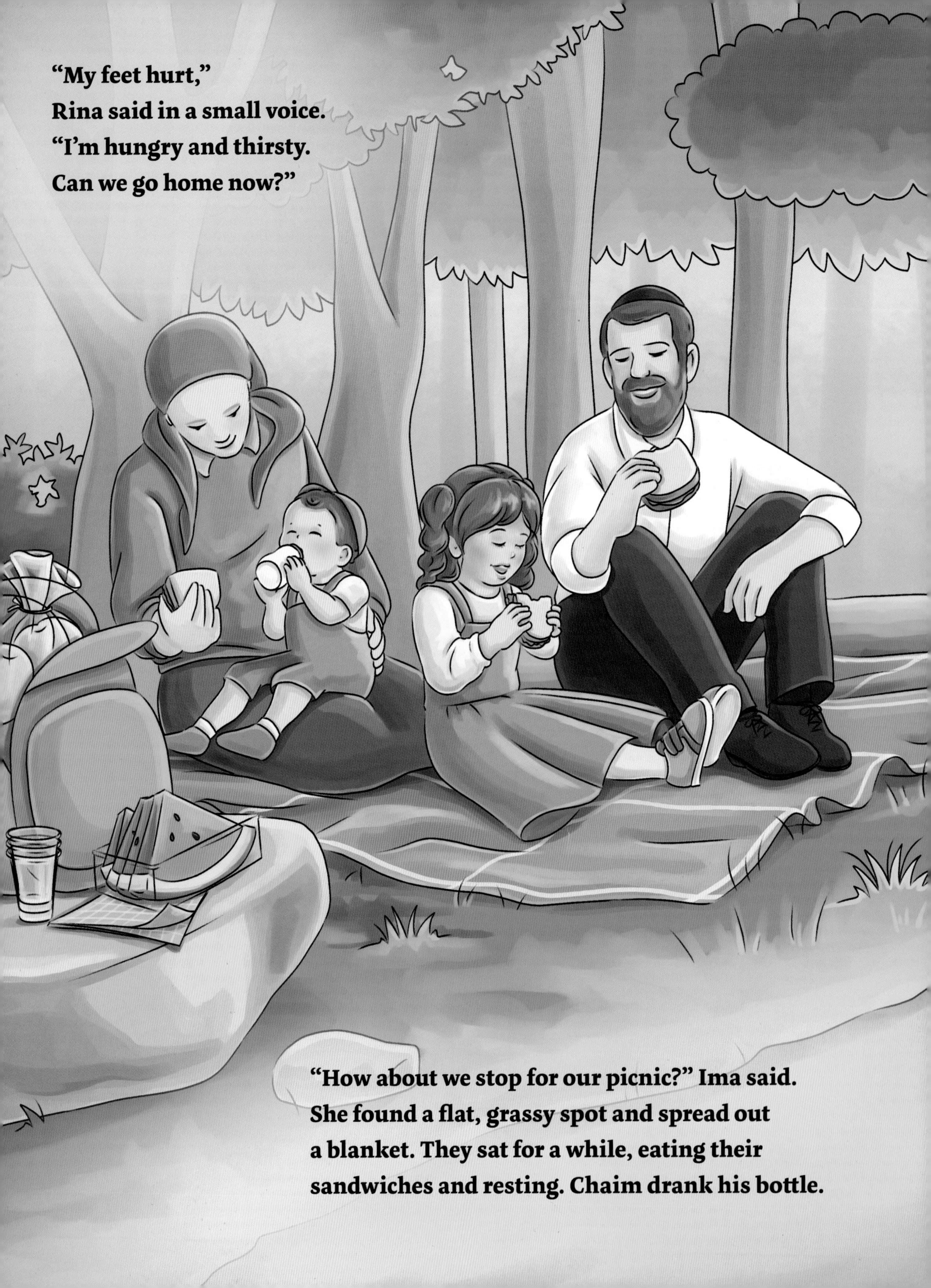

“How about we stop for our picnic?” Ima said.
She found a flat, grassy spot and spread out
a blanket. They sat for a while, eating their
sandwiches and resting. Chaim drank his bottle.

Suddenly, Rina saw a shadow between the trees. She looked up in surprise. Two deer stood there, staring straight at her. They were beautiful. They watched her for a few moments, then turned and ran into the woods.

Rina felt much better.
"I think I'm ready to climb
some more!" she announced.

They continued going up the path.
Rina noticed that she could see more
of the blue sky than before. She
could also see the tops of some trees.

"Are we at the top yet?" Rina asked.

"Almost … You're doing great!" Ima grinned. "You'll know when we're at the top."

And suddenly, there it was. One more step and Rina was out of the forest, standing at the top of the mountain! And Abba and Ima were right — she sure knew it!

Rina took a deep breath and looked around. The view around her was like nothing she had ever seen before.

She could see deep into a valley.

She could see a lake with water that sparkled.
She could even see tiny boats sailing in the water.

She could see trees filled with thick
green leaves swaying in the breeze.

She could see colorful birds flying. She could see a bright blue sky and shiny white clouds that seemed so close she could almost touch them.

She had reached the top of the mountain.

"It wasn't easy to get here," Rina said, thinking of the long climb, the bugs, and her tired feet.

"But it was worth it!"

She thought of the trees, and the chirping. She thought of the birds and the fish. She thought of the deer, and the amazing view. And most of all, she thought of how proud she was of her hard work.

"You did it, Rina!" Abba said. "You're a real mountain climber!"

A Lite girl BOOK
Yael's Loving World
Audio/ Musical CD Included!
by Malky Weinstock

A Lite girl BOOK
New Shoes for Yael
Audio/ Musical CD Included!
by Malky Weinstock

A Lite girl BOOK
Yael Becomes a Giver
Audio/ Musical CD Included!
by Malky Weinstock
Illustrated by Steve Pileggi

A Lite girl BOOK
Yael Worries No More
Audio/ Musical CD Included!
by Malky Weinstock

A Lite girl BOOK
Yael Gets A Guest
Audio/ Musical CD Included!
by Malky Weinstock
Illustrated by Steve Pileggi

A Lite girl BOOK
Yael
and Her New Baby Sister
by Malky Weinstock
Illustrated by Steve Pileggi

A Lite girl BOOK
Yael's Great Big Family
Audio/ Musical CD Included!
by Malky Weinstock
Illustrated by Steve Pileggi

A Lite girl BOOK
Yael and the Shabbos Treats
Audio/Musical CD Included!
by Malky Weinstock
Illustrated by Steve Pileggi

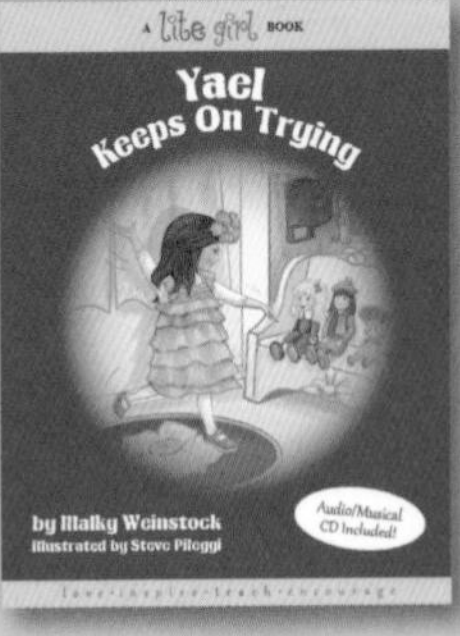
A Lite girl BOOK
Yael
Keeps On Trying
Audio/Musical CD Included!
by Malky Weinstock
Illustrated by Steve Pileggi

A Lite girl BOOK
Yael Plants Seeds
Audio/Musical CD Included!
by Malky Weinstock
Illustrated by Steve Pileggi

A Lite girl BOOK
Yael Stands Tall
A V'ahavta L'reiacha Kamocha story
Audio/Musical CD Included!
by Malky Weinstock
Illustrated by Steve Pileggi

A Lite girl BOOK
Yael and the Secret Language
A story about talking to Hashem
Audio/Musical CD Included!
by Malky Weinstock
Illustrated by Steve Pileggi

A Lite girl BOOK
Yael Learns to Wait
by Malky Weinstock
Illustrated by Steve Pileggi

A Lite girl BOOK
Yael and the Shining Menorah Lights
by Malky Weinstock
Illustrated by Steve Pileggi

A LiteBoy BOOK
Dovy Runs
Audio/Musical CD Included!
LEARN · INSPIRE · TEACH · ENCOURAGE

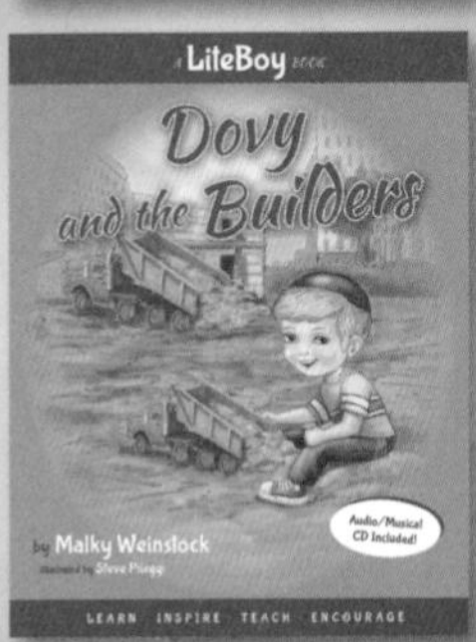
A LiteBoy BOOK
Dovy and the Builders
by Malky Weinstock
Audio/Musical CD Included!
LEARN · INSPIRE · TEACH · ENCOURAGE

A LiteBoy BOOK
Dovy Learns to Share
by Malky Weinstock
Audio/Musical CD Included!
LEARN · INSPIRE · TEACH · ENCOURAGE

A LiteBoy BOOK
Dovy and the Hachnasas Sefer Torah
by Malky Weinstock
Audio/Musical CD Included!
LEARN · INSPIRE · TEACH · ENCOURAGE

A LiteBoy BOOK
Dovy and the Thank You Trip
by Malky Weinstock
Audio/Musical CD Included!
LEARN · INSPIRE · TEACH · ENCOURAGE

A LiteBoy BOOK
Dovy and his Cheer-Up Visitors
A Bikur Cholim Story
by Malky Weinstock
LEARN · INSPIRE · TEACH · ENCOURAGE

A LiteBoy BOOK
Dovy's Special Seder Night
by Malky Weinstock
Audio/Musical CD Included!
LEARN · INSPIRE · TEACH · ENCOURAGE

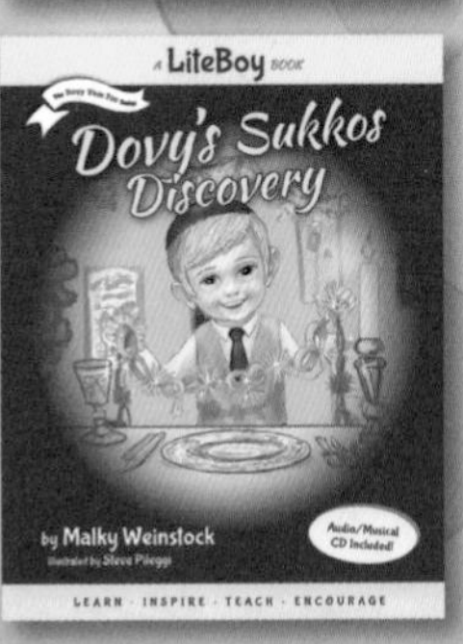
A LiteBoy BOOK
Dovy's Sukkos Discovery
by Malky Weinstock
Audio/Musical CD Included!
LEARN · INSPIRE · TEACH · ENCOURAGE

How
Mitzvah Giraffe
Got His
Long,
Long
Neck
By David Sokoloff

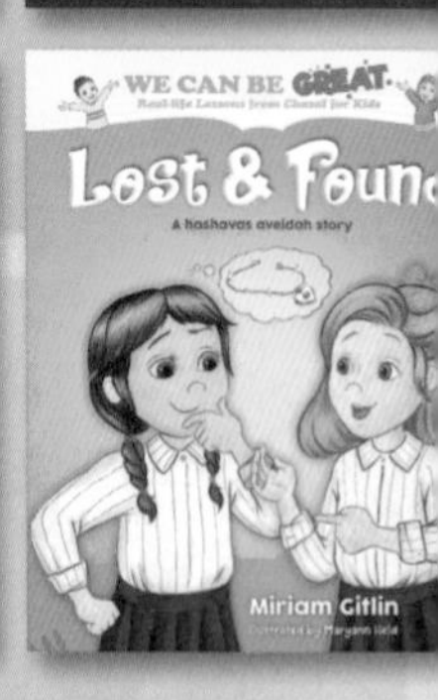
WE CAN BE GREAT
Lost & Found
A hashavas aveidah story
Miriam Gitlin

The Beautiful Brachos Series
Pinny the Plum
and the Brachah
of Ha'eitz
By Batya Cohen · Illustrated by Racheli David

The Beautiful Brachos Series
The Wonders of
Shehakol

SHABBOS
is COMING!
We're LOST
in The
ZOO!
By Devorah Leah
Illustrations by Maya S. Katz

A
Treasure for the
Princess

Wally the Worm
Learns
About KOSHER
Rochel Burstyn

WHERE ARE
MY SHOES?
BY ROCHEL BURSTYN

SPOT THE DIFFERENCE
Shabbos
HOW MANY DIFFERENCES
CAN YOU FIND?
AGES 6 TO 12

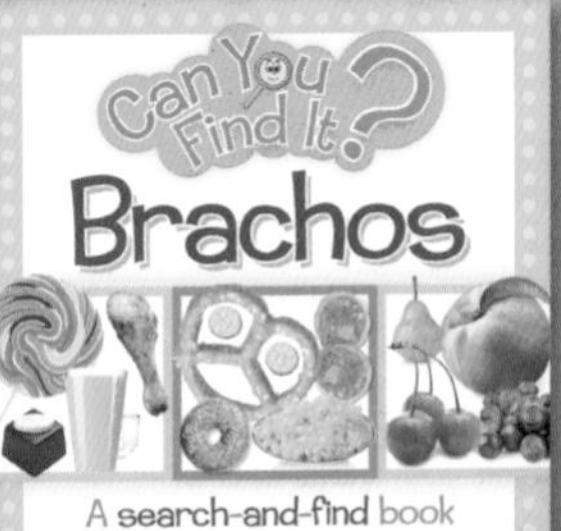
Can You Find It?
Brachos
A search-and-find book

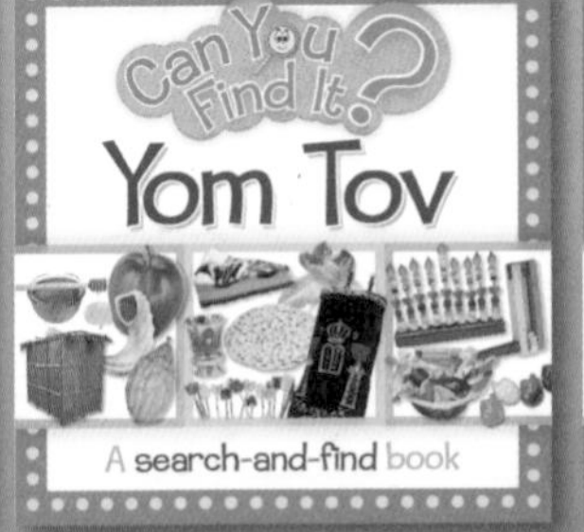
Can You Find It?
Yom Tov
A search-and-find book

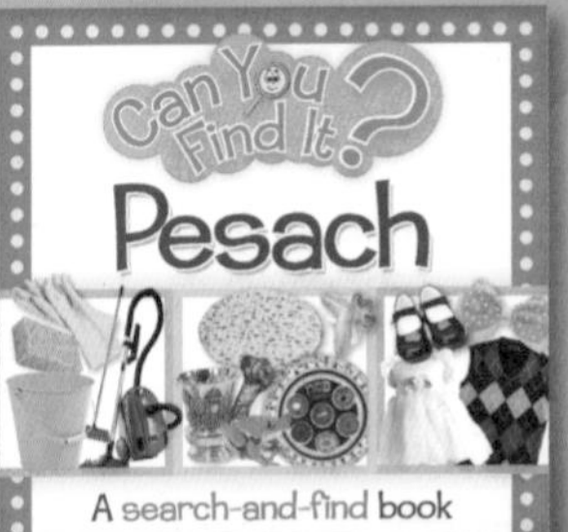
Can You Find It?
Pesach
A search-and-find book

Can You Find It?
Hashem's
Amazing World
A search-and-find book